# Hello, Cat, You Need a Hat

by Rita Golden Gelman

Illustrated by Dana Regan

Hello Reader! — Level 2

SCHOLASTIC INC. Cartwheel ·B·O·O·K·S·®

New York  Toronto  London  Auckland  Sydney

Oh, look.
Just look!
Your head is bare.
I have some hats that you can wear.
Come over here.
I'll give you some.

I do not want one.
Hats are dumb.

I have rain hats...

...hats for sun.

# You'll never catch me wearing one.

Hats for cold with fur and ear things.

Walkie-talkie hats
that hear things.

Monkey hats for getting money.

Hats with nets for getting honey.

Try *this* hat:
You really should.

**If I wanted to, I would!**

Hats to swim in.

Hats to hide in.

Hats to be a groom
and bride in.

You may have *this* hat.
You may.

**I do not want it.
Go away!**

Bands wear hats.
Police do, too.

Teams wear hats.
So why can't you?

Hats for cowgirls.

Hats for knights.

Hats for welding.

Hats with lights.

Hats with chin things.
Hats with spin things.

Hats they give you when
you win things.

I never spin.
I never win.
And I want nothing
on my chin.

Hats for crowning.

Hats for clowning.

Bat hats.
Mouse hats.
Witch hats, too.

If witches wear them,
WHY CAN'T YOU?

Fire hats are best of all.
The way they make the water fall.

Have one.
Have one of your own.

**Get out of here.
Leave me alone!**

Have a helmet hat instead.
A helmet hat protects your head.

**Can't you hear me?
NO! I said.**

Astronauts wear hats in space.

Jockeys wear them in a race.

This one I know
will look just right.

I think we're going
to have a fight.

Oh, no.
Don't fight.
I'll stop.
I will.
Come on.
We'll sit up on the hill.

**Do you mean it?**

Yes. I do.
I will not mention
hats to you.

Oh, look.
Just look!
Your feet are bare.
I have some shoes
that you can wear.
I'll give you some.
Come over here.

**Excuse me while
I disappear.**